A Is for ELIZABETH

written by
Rachel Vail

illustrated by
Paige Keiser

SQUARE
FISH
Feiwel and Frien
New York

SQUARE
FISH

An imprint of Macmillan Publishing Group, LLC
120 Broadway, New York, NY 10271
mackids.com

Our books may be purchased in bulk for promotional,
educational, or business use. Please contact your local
bookseller or the Macmillan Corporate and Premium
Sales Department at (800) 221-7945 ext. 5442 or by email
at MacmillanSpecialMarkets@macmillan.com.

Library of Congress Cataloging-in-Publication Data
Names: Vail, Rachel, author. | Keiser, Paige, illustrator.
Title: A is for Elizabeth / by Rachel Vail ;
illustrated by Paige Keiser.
Description: New York : Feiwel and Friends,
[2019] | Summary: Elizabeth, the second-grade sister of Justin Case,
is excited about her first homework assignment but it leads her
to start a protest of alphabetical order.
Identifiers: LCCN 2018039304| ISBN 978-1-250-25024-7 (paperback)
ISBN 978-1-250-16213-7 (ebook)
Subjects: | CYAC: Schools—Fiction. | Homework—Fiction. |
Fairness—Fiction. | Family life—Fiction.
Classification: LCC PZ7.V1916 Aag 2019 | DDC [E]—dc23
LC record available at https://lccn.loc.gov/2018039304

Originally published in the United States by Feiwel and Friends
First Square Fish edition, 2020
Book designed by Liz Dresner
Square Fish logo designed by Filomena Tuosto

1   3   5   7   9   10   8   6   4   2

AR: 3.2 / LEXILE: HL520L

To Sarah, Katrina, and Becky Ross.
Each first, each best, all fierce and
strong and full of love. —R.V.

For my very good friend, Phyllis —P.K.

Chapter

1

Good news!

Ms. Patel told us today we have homework.

We are in second grade now.

So we get homework!

This is the day I've been waiting for!

The homework is: Make name posters.

Posters of our names!

I raised my hand.

"Elizabeth?" Ms. Patel said, smiling at me.

"Can we make anybody's name we want?" I asked. "In the whole 2B class?"

"No," said Ms. Patel. "You each make your own name."

That news was the opposite of good.

Chapter 2

"Some people have much longer names than other people," I explained to Ms. Patel.

"True," Ms. Patel said.

"Hey! That means some people will have to do more work," Bucky said.

Bucky's name is Bucky.

It has only five letters in it.

My name is Elizabeth.

It has a bajillion letters.

Bucky is my best friend.

"Be creative!" Ms. Patel said. "Have fun making your names!"

"That is not fair," I said.

"Not everything is fair," said Anna, without even raising her hand.

Anna is not my best friend.

Chapter 3

"And Friday, when you bring in your posters, we will hang them all up!" Ms. Patel said.

We all cheered. Class 2B will look so much better covered in posters!

"We will hang them around Class 2B in alphabetical order," Ms. Patel said.

Only some of us cheered at that news.

"Who can remind Class 2B what alphabetical order is?" Ms. Patel asked us. "Hands, please."

Anna's hand was the first one up.

Anna LOVES being first.

"In the order of the alphabet!" Anna yelled.

Ms. Patel hadn't even finished saying the whole name of Anna.

She was still on the *An*.

"Like, first *A* . . ." Anna said.

And she smiled that T. rex smile of hers.

"That's right," Ms. Patel said. "So we—"

"Then *B*," said Anna.

"Yes," said Ms. Patel. "So, we will hang—"

"Then C," Anna said.

"Thank you, Anna," said Ms. Patel.

"You're welcome," Anna said.

Chapter 4

After that, it was time for recess.

Anna was first in line. Of course.

Because of alphabetical order.

When we got to the swings, I
explained to her quietly, "Nobody
likes a show-off, Anna Banana."

Anna shrugged and said, "Sticks
and stones may break my bones, but
names will never hurt me."

Chapter 5

I don't know why sticks and stones
may break Anna's bones.

Maybe Anna is allergic to sticks
and stones.

Bucky is
allergic to
peanuts.

Chapter
6

Anna always gets to be first.

Her name poster will be first.

Also, Anna always gets to sit next to my best friend, Bucky.

All because of the alphabet.

And its order.

And that *A* up at the front of her name.

A is for *Anna*.

A is also for *Annoying*.

Chapter 7

The *E* up at the front of my name, *Elizabeth*, is my problem.

It is the reason I am always stuck between Dan and Fiona.

Dan smells like sneakers and Fiona hardly talks at all.

Recess was done.

I had to line up to go back into
school between Smelly and Silent.

Chapter
8

Today in school, I was still writing my name when everybody else had already finished writing.

Today is Wednesday.

Wednesday is the worst day to write. It has so many extra letters.

Like my name.

My extra letters leaked down the side of my paper.

Now it is Wednesday night.

I have not started my name poster.

Why oh why did those parents name me such a long thing as *Elizabeth*?

Chapter 9

Hooray for today because it is Thursday, and I finally got a great idea for my poster!

There is only one problem with it.

THINGS I AM NOT ALLOWED TO BRING INTO THE HOUSE

1. Sticks
2. Rocks
3. A bad attitude

THINGS I BROUGHT INTO THE HOUSE TODAY

1. Sticks
2. Rocks
3. A bad attitude

Chapter 10

Well.

I had good reasons.

ALPHABETICAL ORDER is the good reason I brought a bad attitude into our house all week.

I did not have a good reason for bringing in the rocks.

Chapter
11

Hang on. I had TWO reasons to bring in rocks.

One of the reasons is a good reason!

The good reason is: decoration.

Decoration is good.

Like on a birthday cake.

Or, if you have time and bubbles,
on your head in the bath.

Chapter
12

The other reason for bringing rocks into the house is a not good reason.

It is the kind of reason that is the opposite of good.

It is because *rocks* means the same thing as *stones*.

And because of the thing that Anna
said about her bones.

Chapter
13

One of the reasons I brought the sticks into the house is a GOOD reason.

It is:

I will make the letters on my name poster out of sticks.

I will glue the letters made of sticks onto poster board.

That is a creative and fun idea!

I will have the best name poster in Class 2B!

Chapter
14

I ran downstairs to tell my parents the exciting news about my project.

"I have homework to do tonight!" I told them. "And I collected the supplies all by myself!"

"What supplies?" asked Mom.

I did not want to get in trouble about the rocks or the sticks.

"Never mind about that," I told her. "All I need now is poster board!"

"Poster board?" asked Dad.

"Yes," I said. "For my homework."

"Elizabeth," said Mom. "It's after dinnertime!"

"The store closes at six p.m., Elizabeth!" said Dad.

"Daddy will have to drive all over Kingdom Come to find poster board at this time of night!" Mom yelled.

"Me?" Dad asked her.

"Woof woof woof!" added our dog, Qwerty.

"What is *Kingdom Come*?" I
asked. "Is that a real place? Are
there dragons in Kingdom Come? Do
dragons like poster board?"

Chapter 15

There is a rule in our family that I forgot all about.

It is:

No saying the words Poster Board after 6:00 p.m.

Chapter
16

"You said it, too," I told Mom.

"Said what?" she asked me.

"The words that rhyme with *toaster sword* . . ."

"Toaster sword?" she asked.

"Yes," I said.

I whispered the words *poster board.*

"You said those words at least five seconds later in the night than I did, Mom."

Mom shook her head.

Dad shook his head.

They both did loud breathing.

That is what they do when I make a good point and win the argument.

Even if there is no trophy involved, I love winning.

I am not a sore winner, no matter what Anna the Annoying says.

I am the opposite of sore.

I am a feel-great winner.

Chapter
17

Dad plucked his keys off the hook
and asked, "Do we need anything else
while I'm out?"

My big brother, Justin, didn't need
anything.

Of course.

"No, thanks," he said.

Mom rubbed his curly hair like he was her good-luck charm.

"Well," I said. "Actually, some strong glue would probably be a good idea."

"Strong glue?" Mom asked.

"To glue my sticks onto the—you know. Thing that rhymes with *boaster floored*." I whispered the last part.

Chapter
18

"Sticks?" Mom asked.

Chapter
19

WHAT I TOLD MOM ABOUT WHY
I AM MAKING MY NAME OUT OF
STICKS:

"Other kids are doing glitter."

Last time I used glitter, Mom said,
"Glitter is a nightmare."

She threw all the glitter in the

garbage, even the glitter that didn't
have glue or our dog in it.

WHAT MOM SAID ABOUT
STICKS INSTEAD OF GLITTER:

"Sticks are a fine idea."

WHAT I DIDN'T TELL MOM
ABOUT WHY I AM MAKING MY
NAME OUT OF STICKS:

The truth.

Chapter
20

I had an idea!
I ran
downstairs.
"Maybe you
could call Daddy," I
said.

"Why?" Mom asked.

"To ask if he can get the biggest piece of *you know what* that they have in the kingdom."

"What kingdom?" Mom asked.

"Kingdom Come," I said.

"That's an expression," Mom said.

"Well, whichever kingdom where he is buying the . . . thing that rhymes with *floaster snored!*"

"There's no kingdom," Mom said.

"So why did you say Daddy was going there?"

"Elizabeth," Mom said. "When did Ms. Patel tell you about this project?"

"Tuesday," I told her.

"Elizabeth!" said Mom. "Today is Thursday!"

x

"I know! I meant to ask every
day, but then, every day? I forgot," I
explained.

"Elizabeth," she said again.

"I'm still new at homework," I said.

"True," Mom said, and she rubbed
my hair.

Sometimes I am her good-luck
charm.

Chapter 21

Mom called Dad.

I danced around, very happy again about my project.

The reason I needed the

most gigantic poster board of all of Class 2B is:

The name *Elizabeth* has a bajillion letters in it!

So maybe I will have the biggest poster in the whole Class 2B!

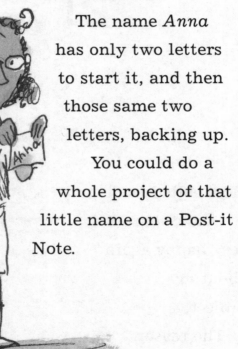

The name *Anna* has only two letters to start it, and then those same two letters, backing up.

You could do a whole project of that little name on a Post-it Note.

Chapter
22

I twirled around my room waiting for Dad to get home from Not A Kingdom.

I tried to make some room on my desk for doing homework.

My brother, Justin, is not the only one with homework now.

I have a new desk in my room.

I have my own set of markers.

I have a great idea.

Soon I will be at the front of everything.

Chapter
23

There was not enough room on my desk.

I spread the sticks and stones out on my rug.

I looked at them.

My dog, Qwerty, looked, too.

I could tell he thought my idea was the opposite of good.

He kept trying to take those sticks away.

Qwerty is a dog.

He has never had homework.

But I was a little bit worrying that maybe he was right, anyway.

Because I kept imagining a very scary thing:

Me in Class 2B tomorrow, holding my poster board with my name made out of sticks and stones.

And then all of Anna's bones, breaking.

Maybe I should borrow Justin's  markers instead.

I could promise to not press so hard
I smoosh their heads in.

I'll ask him.

Anna is a show-off, but I don't
really want all her bones to break.

Chapter 24

Maybe only one small bone.

Maybe just a sprain.

Anna could go to the nurse's office
and sit on the crinkle-paper bench.

She could relax for a while with
her sprained bone.

Instead of smiling all the time right in everybody's face.

Chapter 25

Justin said no to
borrowing his
markers.

He said I
always smoosh
their heads in.

He asked, "Why don't you use your own markers?"

I said, "Because their heads are all smooshed in."

chapter 26

I used the drippy glue Dad bought,
and all my rocks and sticks.

I showed Justin how cool it looked
when I finished.

"You used so much glue," he said.

"I needed it," I said.

"Your sticks are like kayaks in glue ponds," he said.

"They're not kayaks," I said. "They are letters."

"What are you making?" he asked.

"My name," I explained.

"I thought your name was Elizabeth," he said.

Chapter
27

"Sometimes the name *Elizabeth* starts with the letter *A*," I explained to Justin.

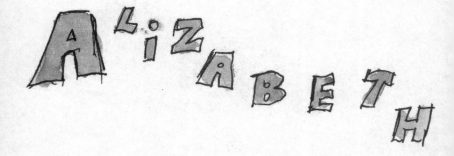

"No it doesn't," he said.

Justin is in fifth grade, so he thinks he knows everything.

"Sometimes it does," I said.

"Never," he said.

"Haven't you ever heard of *sound it out*?" I asked.

Justin looked confused. Ha! Even fifth graders don't know everything.

"*Annoying. Amazing*," I said. "Sound it out. What letter makes the *uh* sound at the beginning?"

"An *A*," Justin said.

"AHA!" I said. "And my name starts with the same sound! *A*-lizabeth!"

"But your name starts with *E*," he said.

"Sometimes," I said.

"Always!"

"Also, sometimes my name has a bunch of *M*s in it. Like a whole little set of mountains."

*M*s take so many of the little sticks.

"No!" Justin said. "There are no *M*s in Elizabeth!"

"Sometimes there are rocks in my name, like this! They are sometimes the dot."

"The dot?" Justin asked. "What even is that?"

"It is called an ex-pla-nation point," I said as my ex-pla-nation.

"Ex-CLA-mation point!" Justin yelled. "It's an ex-CLA-mation point, not an ex-PLA-nation point!"

"Yeah, well, stop explaining, then!" I yelled at him.

He can be very frustrating.

"But, Elizabeth," he said. "Names don't have—"

"I have three of those points in my name," I exPLained.

"No, you don't," said Justin.

"See? I do!" I showed him. "But sometimes the rocks make the letter

O. Sometimes my name has seven *O*s in it."

"No, it doesn't!" Justin yelled louder. "It has zero *O*s! Your name is spelled *E-L-I-Z-A-B-E-T-H*!"

"Sometimes," I agreed.

"ALWAYS! ALWAYS!" Justin shouted. "THAT IS HOW SPELLING WORKS!"

"Maybe for *your* name," I said.

Chapter
28

The poster did not look the way I had
planned.

Some of the sticks and stones had
trouble staying where I put them.

Sometimes I have trouble staying
put, too.

So I get it.

But still.

All Mom and Dad care about is bedtime, even when there is a poster crisis.

Chapter
29

I cuddled up cozy with Dolores, my stuffed dog-rabbit.

Her one eye and my two eyes all stayed open.

We were having trouble with settling down.

The gluey project on my rug was why.

Every time we closed our three eyes, it felt like all the letters got up off my poster and danced around my room together.

While they danced, the stick-letters and the stone-letters sang a song in their teasing sticks-and-stones voices.

The tune didn't matter, but the words kept repeating:

Alphabetical order! Alphabetical order!

Chapter
30

"I thought you were making your name," Mom said at breakfast.

"It is my name," I said.

"But isn't that an *A*?" Mom asked. "And some of those look like exclamation points."

"Don't even try," Justin told her.

"It's an abstract version," I said.

"Oh," Mom said.

"Cool," Dad said.

I felt as unsure as their faces looked.

I said, "We are supposed to be creative in Class 2B."

And I looked as brave as I ever could.

Chapter
31

It was a rough walk to the bus stop.

Not all of my rocks made it.

Luckily, my name is not as strict about spelling as some people's names.

At least the *A* at the start of my name was sticking.

And the other *A* next to that first
A, too.

I needed both those *A*s at the
beginning.

When two names start with the
same first letter, you look at the next
letter.

And think about the alphabet.

That is the rule of alphabetical
order.

Anna has an *N* next to her first *A*.

My name when you spell it
AAbAmmm!moxooo!Eoo'oAth! comes
way before *Anna*.

Because: alphabetical order.

It was okay about the falling-off
rocks.

I didn't need all the *O*s.

Some of them were for decoration.

It's my name.

I should know how to spell it.

"Yes, you should," Justin said.

Chapter 32

My name poster and I needed a bus seat all to ourselves.

My best friend Bucky's poster was rolled up with a red rubber band around it.

His was on the skinnier kind of poster board called oaktag.

He is gentler with markers than I am.

And his mom allows the awesome oily crayon things that ruined our couch.

We don't have those anymore in our family.

Bucky sat in a bus seat with Mallory instead of with me today.

Mallory was in the other first grade
class, so we hardly know her.

Her headband had cat ears on it.

Her poster was rolled up too.

I was starting to feel like maybe I
didn't do it right.

The poster.

Anything.

Chapter 33

I didn't know there was going to be
Tell About Your Poster.

Each kid has to stand up and tell
something.

You can tell a fact about your name.

You can tell about the artwork you
did.

I am not afraid to stand up in front
of the class and say things.

I used to be afraid when I was
little, but I'm not anymore.

Shy is not the reason maybe I
might hide under my desk.

It's that my name looked like it
was melting off my poster.

And Anna's name looked very
pretty on her poster.

Also:

I didn't want to tell the reason I
used sticks and stones.

Chapter 34

Luckily, I had some time while

And then Smelly Dan had their turns telling about their names and posters.

Chapter
35

I didn't listen nicely while the other kids said things.

I didn't come up with a good thing to tell.

Instead I spent my time thinking the word *UH-OH*.

And trying not to hide under my
desk.

Maybe I could tell about the points!

I couldn't remember if it's actually
exPLanation points or exCLamation
points.

Nobody else in 2B had any.

So maybe they really aren't
supposed to be in the middle of our
names.

Maybe my
brother was right.

He had very
strong opinions
about the topic.

"*Elizabeth?*" said
Ms. Patel.

Uh-oh.

Chapter 36

I walked slowly to the front of the room.

I carried my poster board,
decorated in sticks and stones and
dried lakes of glue.

A few rocks fell off along the way.

I was not feeling proud of how that
huge poster looked.

Or of myself for making it.

Chapter 37

I tried to make my mouth say
abstract.

Or *creative.*

Or *A terrible accident on the bus
ride to school.*

No luck.

My mouth stayed clamped shut.

My fingers were making dimples in the poster board.

"Elizabeth?" Ms. Patel said quietly. "Would you like to tell us about your poster?"

A rule in our family is **Tell the truth.**

So I said, "No."

Chapter 38

Ms. Patel smiled kindly at me.

"Do you want to sit down for now?" Ms. Patel asked.

"No," I answered.

"You can have another chance after the other students go," she said. "Maybe you'll get inspired."

I tried to tell my feet to walk back
to my seat.

My feet said NO.

None of me was behaving.

"Elizabeth?" Ms. Patel asked. "Do
you want to take a seat?"

"No," I said.

"Would you like to tell us about your poster, then?" she asked.

"No," I said.

Some of the kids were giggling.

I don't know which kids because I was looking at my poster.

It was a mess.

"Elizabeth," Ms. Patel said.

"It's not fair," I said.

"What's not fair?" Ms. Patel asked.

"Alphabetical order," I said.

Now a lot of kids were giggling.

"Why does *A* always get to be
first?" I asked.

"Yeah," said Bucky.

Bucky is always on my side, even
when he sits next to somebody else on
the bus.

That is why he's my best friend.

"How do you think that makes
the letter *E* feel?" I asked the class.
"Never getting to be first?"

"Or the letter *B*?" Bucky said.

"How about *Z*?" Zora added
quietly.

"Yeah," I said. "Poor Z!"

"Yeah," Bucky said.

"How do you think Z feels?" I asked Ms. Patel. "Always being last?"

"Like the caboose," Zora said.

"What's *caboots*?" Smelly Dan asked.

"A kind of farm in Israel," Cullen said. "My aunt lived on one!"

"Wait," Bucky said. "Why does a Z feel like a farm in Israel?"

"She said *BOOTS*," Mallory said. "*Z* feels like *BOOTS*. Like, down in the mud."

"I don't think *E* and *B* and *Z* feel like anything," Takara said. "They're letters."

"Quiet, please," Ms. Patel said.

Chapter
40

Anna raised her hand. She waggled it around.

"Anna?" Ms. Patel asked. "Do you have a question?"

"No," Anna said. "I have a statement. Or a comment. I think it's a comment."

"Elizabeth is presenting her name poster," Ms. Patel said.

"Well, her poster has no name on it," Anna argued.

"Yes it does," I said. "It has the name *Elizabeth* on it."

Everybody looked at my poster.

Nobody said *Yes, there is her name, Elizabeth, of course!*

Not even Bucky.

Chapter
41

I took a big breath.

"It is unfair that Z never gets to be first, or E, for example," I said. "Other letters should have a turn being first in the alphabetical order."

"Like B!" Bucky yelled. "B always has to be second place. That's not fair!"

"Yeah," a lot of kids said, and told their letters, and how unfair alphabetical order is to them.

Not Fiona, of course. She never says anything.

But a lot of other kids were shouting their first letters.

"Especially Z," Zora yelled.

"See?" I said to Ms. Patel. "Alphabetical order is unfair. That's what I want to say about my name poster. I want to say: This is *not* a name poster. It is a protest sign."

I held my poster above my head.

My friends cheered.

Chapter 42

A protest was not my plan.

My plan was:

My Name Actually Starts with the Letter A! Twice! Surprise! So I Should Be First!

Also, *Sticks and stones may break Anna's bones.*

A rule in our family is: **Stand up for what you believe in**.

WHAT I BELIEVE IN

1. Fairness
2. Take turns
3. Sound it out
4. I want to be first

Mostly, I believe in numbers 1 and 4 from that list.

Ms. Patel is a very nice teacher. She has a quiet voice.

She has crinkles near her eyes and mooshy gooshy arms.

Saying *Alphabetical order is unfair* was standing up for what I believe in.

But saying it to a person like

Ms. Patel, who believes in alphabetical order, is hard.

It made my bones feel like they might all break.

And that's when I realized a terrible thing:

Maybe I am allergic to sticks and stones, too.

Chapter
43

Anna raised her hands again and waggled them around in the air so much.

She was bouncing in her seat saying, "Ooh! Ooh! Ooh! Ms. Patel!"

"Anna," said Ms. Patel.

"Alphabetical order is just the order of the alphabet," Anna said. "Right?"

"Right," said Ms. Patel. "Thank you, Anna."

"You're welcome," Anna said. "Right, Elizabeth? It's just the order of the alphabet?"

"Yes," I said. "Sure."

I was tired, honestly. Protesting is hard work.

"So there is nothing to protest," Anna said. "You can't protest a fact."

"Didn't you ever hear of *take turns*?" I asked her.

"Yeah," Bucky said. "Take turns is a fact, too."

"You might like alphabetical order, Anna," I said. "But it is not fair that *A* always gets to be the first letter!"

"You might *not* like alphabetical order, Elizabeth," Anna said right back. "But not liking a thing doesn't make it unfair."

Chapter 44

Well, true.

But Anna being right did not stop me from wanting to smash my poster board over her head.

Still, I didn't.

Because: *Sticks and stones may break her bones.*

And: *My name (poster) might really hurt her.*

Another rule in our family is: **No hitting anybody over the head with your stuff, Elizabeth.**

So I just stood there in the front of my class, waiting for Ms. Patel to sort this problem out.

Chapter
45

A strange thing was happening in the seat next to my empty seat.

Silent Fiona was raising her hand.

Fiona never raises her hand.

She raised that hand slowly.

She pushed it up into the classroom air, where it had never been raised before.

Fiona's face looked sad about what her hand was doing.

"Fiona?" Ms. Patel asked. "Did you want to say something?"

Fiona didn't answer that question.

Fiona never talks, but she always tries to get the right answer.

I was her math buddy one time in first grade, so I know.

Even when you're Fiona's buddy, you hardly hear her voice.

Fiona closed her eyes and opened her mouth.

Chapter 46

"Maybe it doesn't have to be a conflict," Fiona said.

Her voice was quiet.

But it wasn't shaky.

"What did she say?" Smelly Dan asked.

"Shhh," Bucky told him.

"What do you mean, Fiona?" Ms. Patel asked.

I rested my big poster on the toe of my sneaker because it was getting heavy.

"I don't think we can just say good-bye to alphabetical order," Fiona said.

"Of course not!" Anna said. "It's just a thing. It just *is*."

"All the letters would be in a jumble if we got rid of alphabetical order," Fiona said, a little louder. "The dictionary would be a mess."

"But what about *fairness*?" I said.

"Don't we care about *fairness* and *take turns* in this class?"

"Yeah," Bucky said.

"Fairness!" Zora said.

That made me look down at my poster on my shoe.

It was garbage.

If my original plan had worked, Zora would still be last, like a farm in Israel or muddy boots.

Zora is a smarty-pants, but she is also fun.

She should get a turn being first sometimes, probably.

"But maybe," Fiona said. "Maybe alphabetical order isn't the *only* order."

"We could do height order!" said Babyish Cali, who is shortest in 2B.

"Yeah!" said Mallory, who is tallest.

"Or whose birthday is the highest number," said Bucky.

His birthday is December 31.

"Or the lowest number!" said Smelly Dan.

I don't know when his birthday is, but I have a guess:

Beginning of an early month.

"Or who finishes the math sheet fastest," said Zora.

That is a thing she is *always* first at.

Chapter 47

Everybody had suggestions.

We all yelled them out until Ms. Patel raised *her* hand.

She is the teacher.

The teacher raising her hand?

We got quiet.

"These are terrific ideas," she said.
"Every project needs teamwork to
work."

She got out her fat marker and
huge pad and wrote down all our
ideas.

In just the order we thought of
them.

Chapter
48

We hung up our name signs in an
order called random.

Mine was right in the middle of the back wall.

Ms. Patel said she loves the !s in my name.

I do, too.

We lined up to go out for recess in height order, shortest to tallest.

We lined up for the swings in age order, oldest to youngest.

We lined up to go back inside in curliest hair to straightest.

It was more of a clump than a line

because it's hard to agree whose hair is curliest.

Then we lined up to go to music in a different kind of alphabetical order.

Backward alphabetical order.

Zora was first.

Anna was last.

The music teacher is a bit of a yeller.

So I didn't mind being toward the caboose.

Chapter 49

Turns out a caboose is the last part of a train.

Zora told me during music class.

"I knew that," I said. "I just forgot."

"You thought she said *BOOTS*," Anna said.

"No, I did not!" I said. "That was Mallory who said that! I am the one who said it's unfair that . . ."

"You said a lot of things!" Anna yelled.

"So did you!" I yelled back. "And are you allergic to sticks?"

"No!" Anna yelled.

"Are you allergic to stones?"

"NO!" Anna yelled. "Nobody is allergic to sticks or stones! What are you even talking about?"

"Just making sure!" I yelled. "I didn't want your bones to break!"

"Well, thank you!" Anna yelled.

"QUIET!" Ms. Mooney yelled at both of us.

"You're welcome," I whispered to Anna.

When music was done, we lined up in order of quietest to noisiest.

Fiona got to be the line leader, even though she spoke up today.

She deserved the first spot.

She had been quiet for a long time, before this morning.

Also, she had a really good idea.

Everybody was liking Fiona so
much today.

Including me.

She didn't say anything, leading us
back from music.

But she sure looked proud.

Chapter
50

Anna and I were the noisy caboose together.

It wasn't bad.

Actually, it was the opposite of bad.

Acknowledgments

With thanks and love to:

Amy Berkower, who has long pushed for Elizabeth to have her say

Liz Szabla, who helped me find Elizabeth's punch and rhythm, and propel her to life

Jean Feiwel, feisty and strong like Elizabeth, and thus her guardian spirit

Paige Keiser, who finds (and shows) the soul and heart in each of these characters

The alphabet, for its unrelenting order

Zachary and Liam, first readers forever, whose questions and stories are my always inspiration

Mitch Elkind, who unfailingly believes that a tough, smart girl full of fight and feelings is the best

Mom and Dad, who taught me to share, speak up, and compromise, and also sometimes to not

Carin Berger, awesome at protest signs and glue but even better at friendship

Meg Cabot, hilarious and super-supportive fellow-traveler

Justin Case, worrier, warrior, fictional but so real to me, for introducing me to his awesome little sister

And all the kids and grown-ups who fight—kindly but persistently—to be heard, to defend their friends, and to do what's right

GOFISH

QUESTIONS FOR THE AUTHOR

Rachel Vail

What did you want to be when you grew up?
A spy.

When did you realize you wanted to be a writer?
While I was writing my second book.

What's your most embarrassing childhood memory?
Falling while running for the bus in the clogs I'd sworn to my mom fit me FINE.

What's your favorite childhood memory?
Singing with my family after dinner, any old night.

As a young person, who did you look up to most?
My parents, my cousins, my teachers, and Judy Blume.

What was your favorite thing about school?
Reading.

What were your hobbies as a kid? What are your hobbies now?
As a kid: doing and seeing theater, singing, following the news, pretending. Now: seeing theater, singing, running, hiking, cooking, following the news, yoga, travel.

Did you play sports as a kid?
Yes. I was not as terrible at soccer as I was at softball. But I was world-class terrible at hurdles.

What was your first job, and what was your "worst" job?
First: babysitting. Second: running kids' birthday parties as Tallulah the Clown. Worst: waitress. Not because waitressing is bad, but because I was terrible at it.

What book is on your nightstand now?
I always have a stack! On top right now are: *Black Canary* by Meg Cabot, *An American Marriage* by Tayari Jones, and *Unpresidented* by Martha Brockenbrough.

How did you celebrate publishing your first book?
I bought my parents a rug.

Where do you write your books?
Mostly standing at my kitchen counter, but also sometimes in cafes.

What sparked your imagination for the A Is for Elizabeth books?
After I wrote the Justin Case books, I kept thinking that the character I wanted to hear more from was feisty, confident, emotional, feet-planted, shoulders-squared little Elizabeth. I wanted to know how it felt to be her.

What challenges do you face in the writing process, and how do you overcome them?
The first twenty drafts are always the hardest part for me. I just try to remember that none of it is a tattoo, all of it will be changed, this is the process. Then I go for a run and start again.

What is your favorite word?
Wow.

Who is your favorite fictional character?
Probably Elizabeth. I also love Hermione, Juliet, Falstaff, Septimus Hodge, and Ramona Quimby.

What was your favorite book when you were a kid? Do you have a favorite book now?
I loved every book by Judy Blume and Paula Danziger, and read both *Of Mice and Men* and *A Separate Peace* multiple times. Now—I have different favorites all the time. I am still a voracious reader.

SQUARE FISH

If you could travel in time, where would you go and what would you do?
That might be too political and intense for me to answer right now.

What's the best advice you have ever received about writing?
First drafts are garbage, just get through them without judging. Get something down, so you have something to change.

What advice do you wish someone had given you when you were younger?
Say no when you mean no, and leave when you feel like leaving. Someone else's inappropriate reactions are not your responsibility.

Do you ever get writer's block? What do you do to get back on track?
I get writer's block almost every day. Writing is the only thing for it, even writing about why I can't write this scene. That and getting sweaty doing something else, to quiet my monkey brain.

What do you want readers to remember about your books?
I hope they'll remember feeling astonished, seen, and understood; I hope they'll remember laughing out loud; I hope they'll remember feeling like their

minds were opened a bit while reading. I hope they'll remember loving the stories.

What would you do if you ever stopped writing?
I have so many plans, many of which include reading and travel.

If you were a superhero, what would your superpower be?
I think I'd be Elastigirl.

Do you have any strange or funny habits? Did you when you were a kid?
No. All my habits are and have always been perfectly normal, no matter what anyone told you . . . Who told you?

What do you consider to be your greatest accomplishment?
Phew. Hopefully I haven't achieved it but I guess so far: I've written some books I'm proud of and I've loved and been loved by some very awesome people.

What would your readers be most surprised to learn about you?
Maybe that my pet is a very speedy turtle named Lightning, who wanders free around my apartment like she is a dog.

Want to see more of Elizabeth?

Big Mouth

EL!ZABETH

written by
Rachel Vail

illustrated by
Paige Keiser

Keep reading for an excerpt . . .

Chapter 1

In Class 2B, we are all friends.

We are friends with everybody in the whole class.

It is not easy.

My challenge is Anna.

Also Smelly Dan.

And Babyish Cali.

But mostly Anna.

Chapter
2

This morning, Anna brought a huge, fat book from home for morning reading time.

Anna is a show-off.

Then she whispered to my best friend, Bucky, during lineup to go out to recess.

I made angry eyes at Anna's back
the whole way outside.

She got on the good swing, because
she always does.

I am a fast runner, too, so I got to
the second-best swing.

I pretended I was flying.

I was being Super Elizabeth, who
can fly higher than Ordinary Anna.

I smiled at her, to be nice.

Superheroes who can fly highest
are also polite.

She smiled back.

It was a scary smile.

"WHY IS YOUR MOUTH
BLEEDING?" I asked Anna.

We both dragged our feet to slow
down.

Chapter
3

We got off the swings.

I looked in Anna's open mouth.

Her fingers reached in and came out holding a popcorn, I thought.

"Ooooh! Elizabeth punched Anna!" Smelly Dan yelled, jumping off the slide. "Oooh!"

"No, she didn't!" Bucky said.

"Ewww," Babyish Cali shrieked.
"She's bleeding!"

"Why did you punch Anna?" Zora
asked me.

"I didn't!" I yelled.

"What happened?" Mallory asked,
all calm like a teacher.

Smelly Dan shouted, "Oooooh! I'm

telling! Elizabeth punched Anna in the mouth!"

"I did not," I told him. "Pipe down, you."

This is what I mean about Smelly Dan.

He is always trying to make trouble.